This book belongs to

.....Caroline.....

Copyright © 2016

make believe ideas ltd

The Wilderness, Berkhamsted, Hertfordshire, HP4 2AZ, UK.
501 Nelson Place, P.O. Box 141000, Nashville, TN 37214-1000, USA.

www.makebelieveideas.com

Written by Sarah Phillips.
Illustrated by Stuart Lynch.

Posie

the Kitten in Pink

Sarah Phillips · Stuart Lynch

make
believe
ideas

Posie's the smallest kitten in town.

Her tail is smooth and her paws are round,

but her coat is covered in different patches

of color and pattern – NOTHING matches!

"I'm a fright," moans Posie, "a terrible sight!

A mix and a mess of black, gray, and white,

with splotches and stripes of ginger and brown,

a comical ear, and a crazy frown!"

"Don't be depressed," says Mitch the Mouse.
"Let's go for a stroll toward my house

and have some **fun** with the things we **find**
among **bits** and **pieces** that are **left behind.**"

The **friends** spy something **pink** and **fluffy**,
Long and **thin**, and rather **scruffy**.

Is it a **bird?**

What could it be?

They decide to set the

creature free!

They push and shove
and drag and pull
the heavy can,
but it's too full.

At last it starts to
tip and sway.
Take care!
Keep out of the way!

The **pink** bird-animal is in a heap.
"Perhaps," says Mitch, "it's fast asleep?"

"Maybe," adds Posie,
"we've got it **wrong**,
and it's **no** animal
but a long, long ..."

Wow! Now Posie glitters and glows,
and sparkles from her head to her toes.

Mitch stares and can't believe his eyes.
He hops from foot to foot and cries:

"The Kitten in Pink, that's what you are,
a dazzling, beautiful superstar!
All cats will stop and gaze at you
and follow what you say and do!"

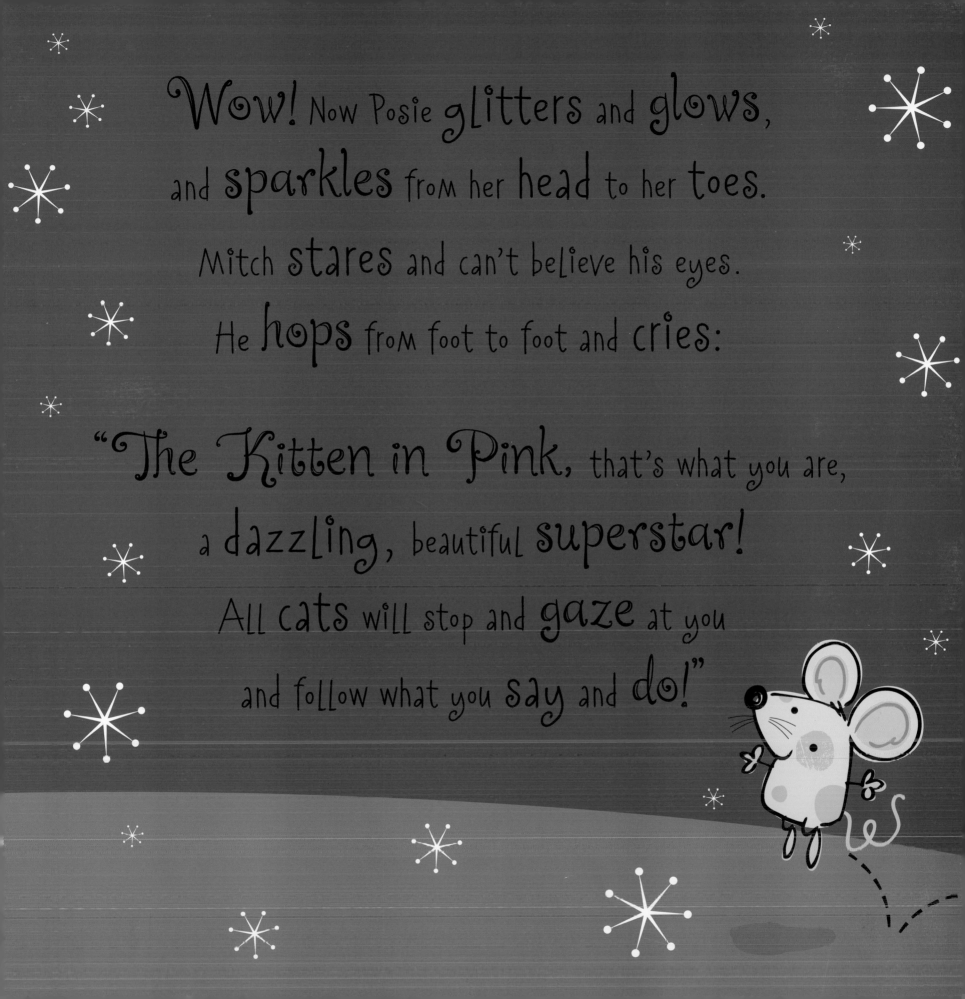

The friends run through the park and see
Little Lil by the big oak tree.

"I've lost my rope; I'm all alone.
It's no fun playing on your own!"

Posie suggests,
"Let's use my scarf
to help Lil skip
and make her laugh!"

The feathers **tickle**, and Little Lil **giggles**;
as she **skips** she **wiggles** and **wriggles**.

They hear a cry as Granny Cat slips
and scatters yarn as she trips.
Three naughty kitties want some fun —
they grab the balls and start to run.

The kitties stare and are filled with shame.

They bring the yarn, and feeling sad,

say sorry to Granny for being bad.

Now Posie thinks and moves at speed;
she wants to help a cat in need.

One thief is caught with
a pink lasso,

while a **yarn** web catches number **two**.

"To thank you," Bob says, "you can take your pick of **any** of my **cakes**."

As **they** start **eating** cakes and pies,
big, black **rain clouds** fill the **skies.**

Rain washes all the glitter away.
Posie was pink for one short day,
but she's happy now and will worry less
that her mixed-up coat is a funny mess.

The **important** thing is what **you** do,
not whether **your** coat is **pink** or **blue**.
Helping those who are **stuck** or **sad**
makes them **happy** and leaves you **glad!**